Penro the Island of Turtles

Su Swallow and Fiona Waters
Illustrated by Catel

Evans Brothers Limited

It is a warm sunny morning and Penrose has decided she needs to spring-clean her boat.

Her two friends are helping her.
Drake the duck scrubs the decks and
Tonga the turtle polishes the mast.

Penrose dusts the picture of her Uncle Roberto.
'Oh Uncle Roberto,' she says.
'Why are you looking at me like that!'

Just then she hears a loud squawk.
She rushes up on deck.
The postman has a letter for her!

Penrose tears open the envelope.

My dear Penrose

I have a special present for you but you will have to find it for yourself. The only clue I will give is that I have hidden it in the middle of an island. An island with lots of eggs but no birds.

Good luck!
Uncle Roberto

'I love surprises,' says Drake.
'Mmm, yes, but first we have to find the island,' sighs Penrose.

Drake unrolls the map.
They look at it long and hard while
Tonga just sits back and watches.
Drake grumbles at Tonga,
'You are not being very helpful.'

'Me? But I know where the island is,' says Tonga, grinning.

Penrose and Drake stare at their friend the turtle.

'It's easy!' laughs Tonga. 'What animal lays eggs but isn't a bird? It is a ... '

'Turtle!' shouts Penrose.
'Hurray! Well done, Tonga!'
And so the three friends set sail
for the Island of Turtles.

Tonga raises the flag.
Drake sets the sail
and Penrose takes the wheel.

The boat sails far across the waves, and that evening, Drake drops anchor off the Island of Turtles. The three friends go ashore.

Several turtles rush to meet them and they all go to the middle of the island.
They stop by a large rock.
'Someone has been digging here!' says Tonga.

'Come on, everyone. Start
digging!' says Drake.
Suddenly, Penrose hits
something hard.
'Stop! I think I have found it!'
Everyone drops their spades.
They brush the earth away
with their hands.

'Whatever is it?' asks
Drake excitedly.
It is huge statue!
'It's a mermaid,' say
the turtles.
'It's a figurehead,' says
Penrose. 'It's to go on the
front of the boat.'
'What a wonderful present!'
says Tonga.
'Yes,' says Penrose,
laughing.
'The mermaid is me!
Uncle Roberto has carved
a statue of me!'

Everyone helps to carry the wooden mermaid down to the shore.

Together they fix the figurehead to the front of the boat. Then it is time to say goodbye.

'Time to go home,' says Penrose as
the three friends set sail
into the sunset, guided by
Penrose the mermaid.